Michael

by Liesel Moak Skorpen
pictures by Joan Sandin

Harper & Row, Publishers
New York, Evanston, San Francisco, London

For our Grandma and Grandpa,
Gyda and John Skorpen

Whenever there was a thunderstorm
Michael and Mud hid under their quilt.

Michael counted slowly to one hundred.
Then he counted slowly back to one.
That was a kind of magic he had made up.
If you counted slowly enough
the lightning couldn't get you.
Mud went under the quilt with Michael
because he liked to be where Michael was.
He wasn't afraid of thunderstorms,
Farm dogs are out in every kind of weather.

Michael's father bawled him out at breakfast.
Michael had left his bicycle out in the rain.
"I put it in the garage," said Michael's father.
"You're not to ride it for a week," he said,
scowling at his eggs.
Michael left most of his breakfast uneaten.
He slammed out of the house.

Michael pushed his hands down into his pockets.
He walked across the field kicking stones.
Mud chased the stones and brought them back,
but Michael didn't want to play.

Mud saw the little rabbit first.
The field was freshly hayed.
The nest was torn.

The mother rabbit must have run away.
There was only one little rabbit left,
too small to run or hide.
Mud licked her gently.
Michael carefully picked her up.
She trembled in his hands.

Michael's father was mowing the lawn.
He had found Michael's baseball glove in the grass
and so he was mad all over again.
"Don't take that thing into the house," he said,
hardly looking at the baby rabbit.
"And wash your hands!" he shouted after Michael.

Michael found a sturdy box.
He lined it with clean hay and new-cut grass,
making a kind of nest in one of the corners.
He set an old window screen across the top.
He wanted to keep the cage in the garage,
but his father said he was cluttering things up.

"This is a pretty good spot," Michael said,
setting the cage by the apple tree.
Mud wagged his tail.

Michael's mother warmed some milk.
She showed him how to test it
on the inside of his wrist.
At first the little rabbit wouldn't suck,
but Michael was patient and very gentle,
and after a while they got the hang of it.
"You'll have to feed her in the night,"
Michael's mother said.
"You'll have to set your clock to wake you up."
"I don't mind," said Michael.

But it wasn't the clock that woke him.
It was the rumble of thunder,
far at first but quickly rolling closer.
Michael pulled up the quilt to cover his head.
"One—two—three," he counted slowly.
Mud crawled under the quilt and wagged his tail.
"Four—five—six," said Michael,
putting his arms around Mud's neck.
Then he remembered about that little rabbit.
"Seven—eight—nine."

He poked out his head and looked at the clock.
It was feeding time.
The rabbit was hungry.
The alarm went off, and Michael jumped.
"Ten—eleven—twelve."

Well, she'd just have to wait until the storm had passed.

"Thirteen—fourteen—fifteen."

Maybe a little rabbit couldn't wait.

Maybe the storm would not let up till morning.

Maybe she'd die.

"Sixteen—seventeen—eighteen—nineteen—twenty."

He wondered if baby rabbits were frightened by thunder.

He wondered if his rabbit missed her mother.

He put on his slicker over his pajamas.
He didn't bother with slippers or shoes.
Michael put his hand on Mud's neck.
That helped a little but not very much.
"Twenty-one—
twenty-two—
twenty-three—
twenty-four."

Thunder rolled and grumbled and growled,
then cracked above them as if the sky would split.
Lightning came in sheets and jagged bolts.
There was lightning everywhere at once.
And rain, driven by a fierce wind,
seemed to be blowing them back to the house.

And then as they reached the apple tree,
the thunder boomed and the lightning blazed
and Michael could see that the screen was down
and the little rabbit was gone.
"Rabbit! Rabbit!" Michael shouted,
though he knew it wasn't any use.
He'd never find her in that drenching dark.

The rain and the wind bent them back toward the house.
A lamp was glowing in the pantry window.
Michael went around to the kitchen door.
The wind was pushing against the door
and he had to tug at it to pull it open.

Michael's father was sitting by the fire.
The lost rabbit was nestled in his arms,
sucking loudly from the little bottle.

Michael's father smiled at him.

"Pretty mean out there," he said.

"Pretty mean," said Michael, shivering.

His father put the empty bottle down.

He held the little rabbit up so they were nose to nose.

"I had a bunny when I was a boy," he said.

"Her name was Nell."

He handed her to Michael.

"That's too much weather for anyone," he said.

"You'd better take her up to bed with you."

Michael put on dry pajamas.
He put an extra blanket on the bed.
He rubbed his head and his feet with a towel
and then he rubbed Mud dry.

Michael's father came upstairs.
"I love you," he said to Michael.
He kissed him good-night.
Mud thumped his tail on the quilt.
"That goes for you too,"
said Michael's father, rubbing Mud's tum.

He would have said good night to Nell
but she was already sound asleep,
safely curled in the crook of Michael's arm.